🌷 A GOLDEN BOOK • NEW YORK

My Name Is Elmo

By Constance Allen
Illustrated by Maggie Swanson

Hello! Elmo is so happy to see you! Welcome to
Sesame Street!
   This is Elmo's room. See outside? There's
Oscar's trash can. Hi, Oscar! And over there is Big
Bird's nest. Hello, Big Bird!

See this hat? It's a firefighter's hat! Maybe when Elmo grows up, Elmo will be a firefighter. Yeah!

This is Elmo's bed. This is Elmo's favorite teddy monster. And this is Elmo's favorite poster.

Do you want to make funny faces? Come on!
Let's make funny faces!

Did you know that furry little red monsters are very ticklish? Tickle Elmo's toes!
Ha! Ha! Ha! That tickles!

Do you want to know Elmo's favorite color? It's yellow! And blue! And red and pink and green and orange and purple! Elmo likes all colors. Yay!

This is Elmo's friend Ernie. Sometimes we play horsie. Wheeeee! Giddyap, Ernie!

Elmo drew a picture. Do you want to see it? Okay! Turn the page and you can see Elmo's picture!

Here it is! See? Maybe Elmo will be a firefighter *and* an artist when he grows up.

Elmo will now show you a trick. Are you ready?
Watch. Are you watching? Okay, Elmo will now
bend over like this . . .

and everything will be upside down! See?
Now you try it.

This is Big Bird. We're friends. Sometimes we try to chase each other's shadows like this.

Here is one of Elmo's favorite games:

Here's Elmo's favorite number: 4. There are four letters in Elmo's name, and four wheels on Elmo's bike. Elmo has four toy cars. And Elmo's pet turtle, Walter, has four feet.

Elmo likes to meet new people. When he
meets them, this is what Elmo says. . . .

Hello! Elmo is so happy to meet you!

ELMO LOVES YOU

A Poem By Elmo

By Sarah Albee
Illustrated by Maggie Swanson

Everyone loves something.
Babies love noise.
Birds love singing.

Kids love toys!

Bert loves pigeons, and pigeons love to coo.
Can you guess who Elmo loves? Elmo loves *you*!

Piggies love to roll in mud.

Penguins love the snow.

Farmers love to wake up early.
Roosters love to crow.

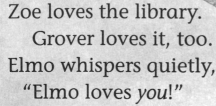

Zoe loves the library.
Grover loves it, too.
Elmo whispers quietly,
"Elmo loves *you*!"

The Count loves counting things.

Ernie loves to drum.

Monsters love
to exercise.

Kids love bubble gum.

Natasha and her daddy love playing
    peekaboo.
But, *psssst!*—before you turn the
    page—Elmo loves *you*!

Monkeys love bananas.

Kids love school.

Grouches love trash.

WHAT A DUMP!

Big Bird loves the pool.

Everyone loves something.
Elmo told you this was true.
And now you know who Elmo loves:
Elmo loves *you*!

Before he ends his poem, Elmo wants
    to ask you this:
Will you be Elmo's valentine?
Could Elmo have a kiss?

The Monsters on the Bus

By Sarah Albee
Illustrated by Joe Ewers

The wheels on the bus go
round and round,
round and round,
round and round.

The wheels on the bus go
round and round,
all through the town.

The baby on the bus cries,
  "Waah-waah-waah!
  Waah-waah-waah!
  Waah-waah-waah!"

The baby on the bus cries,
  "Waah-waah-waah!"
all through the town.

The parents on the bus say,
  "Shhh-shhh-shhh,
  shhh-shhh-shhh,
  shhh-shhh-shhh."

The parents on the bus say,
  "Shhh-shhh-shhh,"
all through the town.

What a cute baby.

The wipers on the bus go
swish, swish, swish,
swish, swish, swish,
swish, swish, swish.
MONSTER NEWS
Excuse me, sir, but your umbrella is dripping on my magazine!

The wipers on the bus go
swish, swish, swish,
all through the town.

A monster on the bus says,
"Coo-ooo-kies!"
all through the town.

The radio on the bus goes
Boom! Boom! Sha-boom!
Boom! Boom! Sha-boom!
Boom! Boom! Sha-boom!

The radio on the bus goes
Boom! Boom! Sha-boom!
all through the town.

The frogs on the bus hop
up and down,
all through the town.

The cows on the bus go,
Moo-oo-oo!
Moo-oo-oo!
Moo-oo-oo!

The grouches on the bus go
Bam! Bam! Bam!
Bam! Bam! Bam!
Bam! Bam! Bam!

The grouches on the bus go
Bam! Bam! Bam!
all through the town.

The band on the bus plays
Oom-pah-pah!
Oom-pah-pah!
Oom-pah-pah!

The band on the bus plays
Oom-pah-pah!
all through the town.

HIM again?

The Martians on the bus go,
  "Yip! Yip! Yip!
  Yip! Yip! Yip!
  Yip! Yip! Yip!"

The Martians on the bus go,
"Yip! Yip! Yip!"
all through the town.

The bird on the bus sings
"La! La! La!
La! La! La!
La! La! La!"

The monsters on the bus all
  wave good-bye,
  wave good-bye,
  wave good-bye.

TAXI!!!!!

The monsters on the bus all
  wave good-bye,
all through the town.